Patch and Ruby

For T, my 'mooseling' and inspiration. – AJ

For Meg, a great friend to ponies and Dutton. – GJ

First published 2016

EK Books
an imprint of Exisle Publishing Pty Ltd
'Moonrising', Narone Creek Road, Wollombi, NSW 2325, Australia
P.O. Box 60–490, Titirangi, Auckland 0642, New Zealand
www.ekbooks.org

A CiP record for this book is available from the National Library of Australia.

ISBN 978-1-925335-22-4

Designed by Big Cat Design
Typeset in Warnock Pro 20/33pt
Printed in China

This book uses paper sourced under ISO 14001 guidelines from well-managed
forests and other controlled sources.

10 9 8 7 6 5 4 3 2 1

Patch and Ruby

Anouska Jones

Illustrated by Gwynneth Jones

Patch was lonely. It wasn't that he didn't have friends. He did. But sometimes he felt like he didn't quite fit in.

Each day, after breakfast, he
hung out with Beryl and the girls.

But they never stopped gossiping.

Around lunchtime, he liked to check on the veggie patch with Lily and her family.

But Lily didn't always appreciate his efforts at gardening.

In the evenings, he ate dinner with Ernie and Edith.

But they were often pretty busy looking after the kids.

And whenever he could, he loved
spending time with his special girl, Sam.

But she had school to go to and other friends to play with.

Then one day, Sam had an idea …

Patch was quietly grazing when he heard
a horse trailer pull up. Out walked ...

Ruby!

Patch and Ruby eyed each other.

Patch and Ruby circled each other.

Patch neighed and stamped his hoof.

Ruby snorted and tossed her mane.

Then Patch walked up ...

... and, ever so gently, touched his nose to hers.

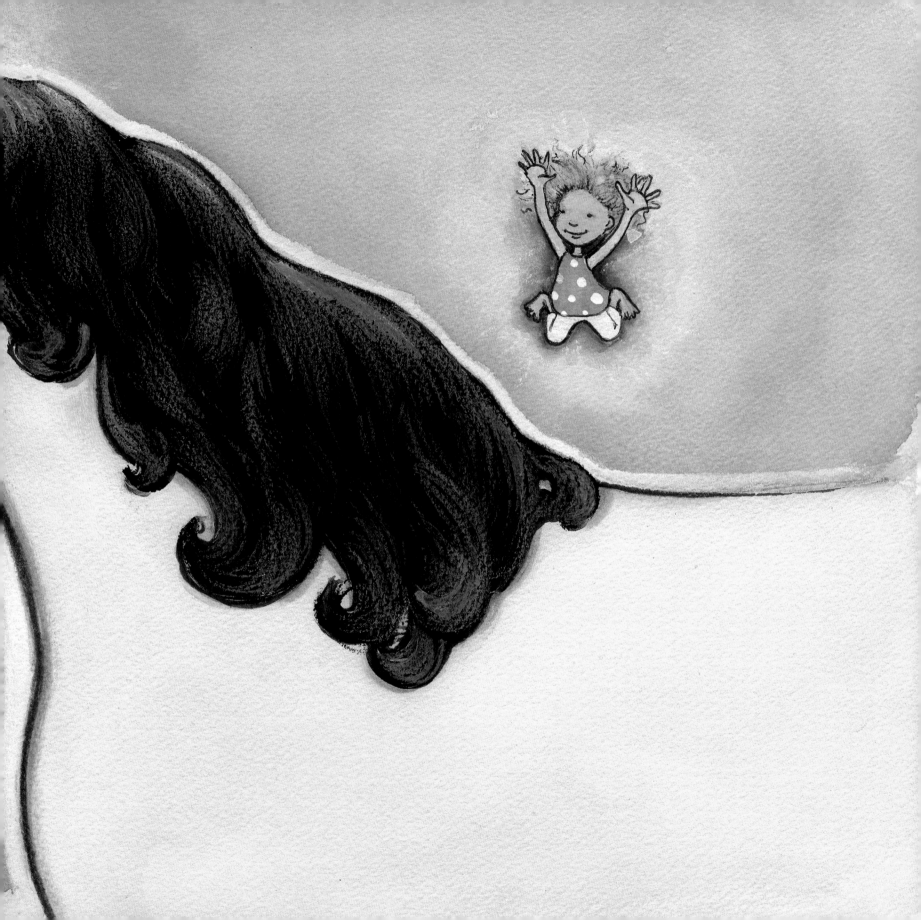

Now life is different.

Each day, after breakfast, Patch and Ruby
drop in for a chat with Beryl and the girls
before enjoying a nap in the sun.

Around lunchtime, they like to weed the veggie garden under Lily's watchful eye.

In the evenings, Patch and Ruby share dinner together

while Ernie and Edith get ready for a night out.

And whenever they can, they spend time with their special girl, Sam.

Patch and Ruby.

Now everything is just right.